The Adventures of (Kronta) Redflower and Betsy

JONATHAN BEARD

PAGE PUBLISHING
Conneaut Lake, PA

First originally published by Page Publishing 2024

ISBN 979-8-88960-873-8 (pbk)
ISBN 979-8-88960-889-9 (digital)

Printed in the United States of America

In the old days way out West, two young girls quickly became good friends.

Redflower was a Native American Indian kicked out of her tribe because they thought she was a living curse. From then on, she had to live on her own.

Betsy, a nine-year-old former slave, was headed out West on a wagon train with a group of other fellow former black slaves. One day, suddenly, a group of masked horsemen attacked the poor slave wagon. "Run, Betsy!" said her grandfather. "Save yourself!" Sadly, the horsemen showed no mercy. They assaulted the slaves with deadly force. It was truly an unfriendly act.

Everyone died except poor Betsy as she watched the slaughter. The carnage and butchery were ruthless. The cowardly horsemen spared no one. The poor slaves were just freed before tragically being killed. Though they worked in bondage, they died as free people.

Betsy cried and cried all night long. She didn't eat or sleep. She just stayed next to her dead grandfather. But thirst is greater than hunger, so Betsy left to find water. Eventually, she made her way back to the ashes of burnt wood that were once a wagon train. There, Betsy saw a stranger, a young Indian girl. In the stranger's hand was the watch of Betsy's grandfather.

Betsy shouted, "That's my grandfather's watch! Give it back to me!"

"Okay," said Redflower. "I don't need your watch. I can tell time by the setting of the sun. Here, take it."

Now as Redflower started to walk away, Betsy cried out, "I'm lost! Take me with you!"

"No," said Redflower. "I don't need you. I can live all on my own."

"But I can't!" cried out Betsy. "Please don't leave me here all by myself. I will die out here! I need you to protect me. You're older than me."

"No, I said!" Redflower replied. "I am Kronta, and I live alone." (Translated in English, *Kronta* means "Redflower.")

But Betsy continued her cries for help until Redflower's heart softened. Redflower was moved by Betsy's innocence and helplessness and felt a gentleness about Betsy. In no time, the two would bond. But Redflower would set down some rules for Betsy.

First, Redflower told her, "You are right. I am older than you. Therefore, you will do what I say. If I say, 'Let's move,' then you move. If I say, 'Don't move,' you don't move. I will take care of you and show you how to hunt and find food, but you must let me lead. Now speak! Do you understand?!"

"Yes," Betsy humbly said. "By the way, my name is Betsy. How old are you?"

Redflower replied, "Sixteen."

So here we have it, a sixteen-year-old and a nine-year-old left to fend for themselves.

Betsy would always have a telltale when something dangerous, shocking, or significant happened. She would always be short of breath and her eyes wide open. As Redflower came to know Betsy, Redflower would realize Betsy's tells.

And so they set off. As they walked for miles and miles, Betsy soon got tired. "Let's rest," said Betsy.

"Soon, very soon," said Redflower. "We have to cover a lot of ground. We are in the Ca'tuck territory. They spare no one who comes into their land. Walk quiet, make no sound. Too much noise will arouse their attention. We don't need that."

"But I'm so tired and sleepy," said Betsy.

"Me too," said Redflower. "But we have to go on. Don't worry. I'll lead us to safety."

At that moment, Betsy realized Redflower was a leader. Because she would help Betsy to freedom and from harm or danger. Redflower would become her friend, protector, and lifeguard.

Eventually, Redflower and Betsy would reach a frigid, high mountain place. Near the top, there was a cave. But Redflower was very cautious. Not taking any chances, she slowly walked into the cave. All she found were old dried-up animal bones.

"Come on in here," shouted Redflower. "It is safe. I'll make a fire to keep us warm."

"Yes, Redflower," said Betsy. "And let's get something to eat as well."

Patiently, Redflower replied, "Look, Betsy, it is late, and we need to rest here. I have a little meat in my pouch. Here, take this and eat, and then I want you to go to sleep, Betsy. We have a very long day ahead of us."

"Yes, Redflower," Betsy meekly said. Moments after putting the dry meat into her mouth, Betsy cried out, "Hey! This meat tastes funny! I don't like it, Redflower!"

Suddenly, Redflower became angry.

"How dare you complain about the food I gave you! I should have eaten it myself! Maybe the little black girl should hunt for food herself!"

"Look, don't call me that," Betsy shot back. "I don't like it. Don't call me a little black girl! My name is Betsy."

"Yes, I know. And my name is Redflower. Don't forget it. I took you in, led you out from the Ca'tuck territory, found this cave for us, and all you can do is complain. Is that how you repay me?"

"I'm sorry, Redflower," said Betsy. "You were right. You took good care of me. I should be grateful…very thankful. Hey, look see! I'm eating the meat! See! Down it goes! Redflower see?"

Having embarrassed herself, Betsy wanted very much to please Redflower. But Redflower was still upset with Betsy.

"If you think saying sorry will make me feel better, forget it! All I want you to do is to go to sleep," said Redflower.

"But, Redflower, can't we talk about it to clear things up?"

"No, I told you to go to sleep."

"Yes, Redflower, I'll go right to sleep now. But let's talk when daylight comes, okay?"

Now as the two lay sleeping, a wild animal entered the cave with bad intentions. With flames in his eyes, he was up to no good. Suddenly, he came at them with a fury truly to do them harm.

But Redflower moved with lightning speed. The wild animal had no idea she could move so quickly. Swift and sudden was Redflower. Before the animal knew it, Redflower had picked up a rock and hurled it at him with great force as the animal fell to the ground.

Redflower could tell the wild animal was in deep pain. So she asked him, "Does it hurt?"

The wild animal cried out.

"Good," said Redflower. "I want it to hurt." Again she struck him with a rock. "Does it hurt?"

The animal cried out in pain once more.

Redflower went into a frenzy. She had gone nearly mad doing away with this invader. In the mind of Redflower, this wild animal entered her cave forcefully as an enemy who would do harm to a person. But the invader messed with the wrong person.

As she continued to administer great pain to the wild animal, Betsy prayed Redflower would stop.

"Enough, Redflower!" said Betsy. "Let us leave this place."

"Get out of my way," shouted Redflower. "Stand back against the wall! And don't you move, Betsy!"

"Redflower! Redflower! Stop what you're doing! Enough is enough."

With maniacal laughter, Redflower looked at the animal and said, "You're not dead. You're acting like you're dead because you don't want the physical punishment that you rightfully deserve. You're faking, aren't you? You might fool Betsy but not me. Get up and crawl out of here like a whipped dog. Or I'll give you more."

The animal gave her a look as if to say, "Please don't hit me anymore. Don't hit me anymore. I don't want any more pain."

Then Redflower said, "You should have thought of that before you came into my cave with bad intentions in your heart."

"Please," said Betsy. "Let the animal go. He is hurt too badly to do us any harm. Leave him. Redflower, let us go."

"You're right Betsy, let's move on. I'll make him feel more hurt if he tries to harm us again. I wish this animal could speak so he can say it hurts."

As the two girls walked away, it was still dark, and they needed rest. Betsy, being the youngest, got tired much faster. But Redflower told Betsy to keep up and not to stop at all.

"Please, Redflower, I'm exhausted. Can't we rest a bit soon?" Betsy said.

"We're almost there," said Redflower. But Redflower, having compassion for Betsy, put her arms around Betsy to comfort her because she knew Betsy was worn out from walking so long. Soon, Redflower led Betsy to a wooded area and a place to hide. For Betsy was very tired and needed rest.

"Sweet dreams, Betsy. See you in the morning," Redflower tenderly said as she made a bed for Betsy to go to sleep. Both could rest now. The night was cool and just right for sleeping.

The next morning, Betsy could smell something nice to eat. Redflower had gotten up early to make breakfast. This time, it was a meal that they both could enjoy. Redflower caught a desert hen as it came into the woods for seeds and water. As Betsy's eyes gazed upon the roasted hen, her lips smacked with delight, ready to eat.

Betsy ate it and said, "It is so good! I want to learn to hunt just like you. Teach me, will you?"

"I will, Betsy, but you can't learn in one day. It will take some time. Didn't I tell you I'll take care of you?" Redflower replied.

"Yes, you did. And so far you've kept your promise," Betsy said.

"Now after you eat, I want to show you how to use a spear and, most importantly, how to throw it. Someday you might need it," Redflower said.

"Yes, Redflower," said Betsy.

Redflower's spear was made out of a long wooden piece cut from a tree branch. She then took a knife and carved a pointed head to make a sharp edge. This weapon made her a true female warrior.

Redflower gained experience in fighting battles because her tribe were fierce warriors. She learned how to fight from them. And now she would show Betsy how to defend herself.

As the days went by, Betsy also became quite skillful with the spear. She even mastered how to throw it with accuracy so as not to let prey escape from her. Redflower, the girl who mastered living in the wilderness, proved to be a great instructor. Redflower would teach Betsy lessons she would never forget until the day she grew old and was put in the ground.

Now one day, Betsy went deep into the forest. Suddenly, she exclaimed, "A baby cub!" She could not help herself and began to play with the cub. Unknown to Betsy, the mother bear was very nearby.

Betsy suddenly caught sight of the she-bear and immediately took off, running to save herself. Fast were her feet. In a flash of lightning, she returned to Redflower with a strange look on her face.

Redflower said, "Why are you sweating and breathing so fast? Your eyes are wide open."

"Well you see…this thing," Betsy sheepishly said.

"What thing?" shouted Redflower.

"A bear," Betsy muttered.

"A bear? What have you done?" Redflower incredulously exclaimed.

Betsy was too embarrassed and scared to tell Redflower the truth, so she said, "Nothing. I've done nothing at all."

Before Redflower even had time to respond, she looked up and saw the she-bear coming straight at them.

"Run! Head to the river where it is deep!" Redflower hurriedly said.

Redflower knew of an underwater cave.

"We must go by the long log that is trapped along the bank in the water. We will dive there and hope the bear doesn't follow us."

Before Betsy's blunder, Redflower had gone fishing; she was preparing a meal for the two of them after having a very successful day. But now as they ran toward the river, Redflower and Betsy could only look on from the water as the she-bear stopped and devoured their food, not leaving a single scrap.

As they lifted their heads above the water, the current became strong. Betsy held on to Redflower's arms for dear life.

Betsy said, "I think we're safe. Well…there goes our food, Betsy! I hope you're not hungry. Because it looks like we're not eating tonight!"

Redflower was in no mood for jokes or laughter. Redflower's long black hair usually resembled a raven's beautiful dark feathers, but at that moment, the water had made her hair disheveled and strewn all over her face. Betsy used her hands to gently sweep the hair out of Redflower's eyes.

As the two held on tight to the log in their tiny refuge, Betsy noticed how stern Redflower looked. Redflower had a fierce glare that could pierce the defenses of a Ca'tuck warrior. Betsy, knowing she had made a mistake, tried to assuage the anger and tension with idle conversation.

Redflower said, "Don't speak to me right now, Betsy. I'm very upset with you. Maybe I'll change my mind in the morning. Come, let us swim toward the shore. It's getting dark, and I want you to go to bed. Don't give me any lip. I don't want to hear it from you all night."

"Don't be mad at me, Redflower," Betsy pleaded.

With very little energy and patience left, Redflower replied, "Hey, I told you to shut up. Don't try to soften me up. It won't work. All I want from you is to close those eyes and sleep."

Betsy knew that she messed up, so her best bet was to comply with the wishes of Redflower.

After a while though, Redflower did soften up and said, "I am so upset with you for getting us into this mess. You should have left that baby cub alone! A mother bear like that will kill us! Her claws could rip us in half with one swipe. You need rest. I will talk to you when daylight comes."

After a good night's rest, Redflower felt contrite for yelling at Betsy. She realized that Betsy was young, innocent, and didn't have any experience in the wild.

"Get up, Betsy. Come let us find food. Here, I made you a spear of your very own. We will hunt deer today. Watch me and learn." The spear Redflower made was beautifully adorned with colors, feathers, and paint. Betsy smiled from ear to ear knowing that Reflower was no longer upset.

Betsy was famished from missing dinner the previous night, so it was time to hunt. Betsy wanted very badly to learn how to hunt on her own. She envied the way Redflower would effortlessly take down huge beats and dismantle them to eat.

"Hide behind that tree," Redflower instructed. "That deer is going to come right at us. Don't let it see us. Stay out of sight."

As the deer got near, Redflower rubbed two sticks together, mimicking the sound of two deer fighting. The sound began to draw the deer even closer. Confidently, Redflower aimed her spear and threw it with a swiftness and strength that frightened Betsy. Down the brown deer went. The spear had found its mark. Today the young females would eat well, and the hide would make a durable set of clothes for their bodies.

Betsy, driven by a visceral hunger, began to devour the meat as soon as Redflower finished cooking it.

Redflower, unable to contain her laughter, said, "Slow down, Betsy, before you choke yourself. That meal isn't going to get up and walk off."

Now as the two enjoyed their meat, they suddenly heard a piercing howl. It was Scarface, the one-eyed wolf—Redflower's old enemy. Redflower had battled Scarface before when he had two eyes. After a tangle with Redflower, he was left with only one.

Even with one eye missing, this wolf still was very dangerous.

Scarface smelled the meat but feared the campfire the girls had set up. However, feeling the pangs of hunger, he would do what was necessary to get a taste of that deer meat. He had gradually come closer to the two girls, who had led their guard down to eat. As Scarface's hunger intensified, he was no longer afraid of the campfire.

Redflower's spear was out of reach and so was Betsy's after having laid the two spears by a tree to clean the deer that they had killed. There was no way they could reach the spears in time. What would they do?

Well, Redflower was no amateur. Hidden in her bosom was a sharp knife. She pulled it out and then said to Betsy, "Another lesson, Betsy. Never be without a weapon! Let's spread out! Pull out your knife, too, and we will catch him off guard. He can't bite us both if we're in different places. One of us will get him."

But as soon as the two young brave girls were about to put their plan into motion, Scarface sensed he would be overmatched. And so he ran, thinking it better to have hunger but keep his life. He would try again later, on his terms, when the time was right.

Now the girls could enjoy the meat without the likes of Scarface.

"How does it taste?" Redflower nervously questioned.

"Good," replied Betsy.

"I like it too," Redflower said behind a smile.

The delicious meat soon made the two of them feel content and drowsy. Both of them fell fast asleep.

The next day, Redflower got up early to get some water. Fresh water was a long way from the camp. The shortest distance was through the brush. However, camouflaged in the brush was a deadly Neltada snake. Unaware of it, the snake struck its mark: Redflower's heel.

Feeling the immediate effects of the snake's deadly venom, Redflower's body began to seize and convulse. Now, all Redflower could do was yell out, "Betsy help me! I've been bitten by a snake!"

Betsy, still groggy from overeating, woke up from her slumber. She had never heard such fear in Redflower's voice. Betsy raced to Redflower's aid.

"You must be brave!" Redflower choked out in between waves of pain. "There's a plant, a Gee-Gee plant. It is bright orange in color. You will know it when you see it. It is a plant unlike any other. It will help make me well. You must go and get it. Go to the south about half a mile. Follow the water stream. Look for the big rock shaped like a human face. There, you will find the Gee-Gee plant growing among the fungus fields. You must be quick before the poison spreads throughout my body."

And so Betsy ran as fast as she could to get the Gee-Gee plant. As Betsy calmed down and settled into her sprint, she remembered some of Redflower's lessons. *Never go anywhere without your weapon.* So Betsy took her spear with her.

Betsy followed Redflower's directions carefully. The Gee-Gee plant was there, just as Redflower said. Briefly distracted by its beauty, Betsy ripped out three Gee-Gee plants and turned to run back to Redflower.

Suddenly, Betsy felt a mighty blow to the side of her abdomen. Betsy fell to the ground but managed to recover quickly. She looked up; it was Scarface. With fire in his eye and his large fangs ready to rip her open, Betsy was not ready for battle with Scarface. However, she needed to be ready to help her friend.

She readied her throwing stance to hurl her spear. Then she thought to herself, *If I miss, Scarface will have me at his mercy.* Betsy noticed a perfectly sized rock that she could throw first. If she missed, she would still have her spear. As Betsy slung the rock, it met Scarface's nose head-on. He screamed in agony with a shrieking howl. Then Betsy remembered Redflower's old saying, and she imitated her. "Does it hurt?" she shouted to Scarface. The wolf wasted no time in retreating. Down to one good eye, this wolf now only wanted to quickly find a place of refuge to ease his pain. Betsy laughed at how cowardly Scarface looked. Now she and Redflower had both defeated him.

Not forgetting the trouble Redflower was in, Betsy had to hurry back to her friend. If something happened to Redflower, Betsy would never make it on her own in the wilderness. Betsy moved expeditiously along the path.

Redflower, now feverish and nearly delusional, looked at an object speeding right at her. She readied her weapon. But wait! It was Betsy with the Gee-Gee plant.

Redflower immediately said, "Give it to me, and I'll prepare it for my heel."

Redflower's forehead had sweat rolling down it as if she had been caught in the rain. She was in pain. But the Gee-Gee plant worked just in time. After a while, Redflower regained her strength. Betsy had never felt so relieved. Betsy wasn't finished learning lessons from Redflower. Without her, Betsy wouldn't survive very long in the wilderness.

Soon, Redflower had enough strength to sit up and she said, "I'm hungry Betsy!" with a smile. This time, it was Betsy's turn to get Redflower something to eat. Before you knew it, Redflower was walking around. She was her old self again.

The day came when Redflower and Betsy needed to cross the River of Wind. Redflower had taught Betsy many things, but in Betsy's mind, she had been a great swimmer long before she met Redflower. Betsy would boast about her swimming skills. Frankly, Redflower got tired of Betsy's big mouth. So one day, Redflower said, "Hey! Show me how good you are. There is the Zharhoush River, the swiftest in the land! I'll cross it first, then you follow me."

"No problem!" said Betsy. "I know what I can do."

"Yeah? We shall see. Let the great Betsy show me how good she is."

And so they set off to the river. The Native Americans call it the River of Wind because the strong gusts of wind near it never stop. Despite the strong wind, it was a bright sunny day when Betsy and Redflower arrived. You could smell the water in the summer air. Redflower's long black hair was flowing in the wind. Her hair smelled of Rosemary oil and Yucca.

Now as they got near the river, Betsy turned white. She had lost her confidence. She thought to herself, *I had better not swim right now.* So Betsy said, "Actually, I'm not in the mood to swim. Let's do something else. We can go around the river."

"Oh no, you don't," said Redflower. "We're going to do it. If I go into the water, then so will you. If you don't, I'll make it very tough for you. Don't play games with me, Betsy. You shot off your big mouth. Now I'm going to hold you to it. This is your next lesson."

Betsy stammered, "Okay, Redflower. I'm not scared. But you go first."

Redflower said, "I will. But when I looked back, I had better see you behind me."

Now it was time to put up or shut up. Redflower took off her moccasins and tied them around her neck, then she gracefully dived into the water. The current was strong, but Redflower was stronger. After living alone in the wilderness, battling Scarface, and nearly dying of snake venom, a river current wouldn't take Redflower down. She made it to the other side. Soaking wet, Redflower looked across the water and shouted, "Your turn, little black girl!"

With indignation, Betsy said, "I *detest* when you call me that! Stop it!"

"Well just dive in! I'm here on the other side waiting for you. No more excuses! Just do it!" shouted Redflower. "I went into the water Betsy, so it's your turn."

Feeling embarrassed, Betsy angrily jumped into the water. She shot off like a steam-powered boat, going quickly but not pacing herself. Redflower was impressed, but she would never tell Betsy.

Just as everything looked alright for Betsy, she began to tire. Fatigued, Betsy yelled, "Redflower, I can't make it. Save me. I don't want to drown!"

"Swim, swim!" Said Redflower. "You can make it! I know you can! I won't let you drown!"

"I'm so tired. I can't make it Redflower. Do something! Please! I can't make it," Betsy pleaded.

"Yes, you can! Yes, you can!" Redflower encouraged. "You're almost there, give me your hand. You're just a few feet away from me. Stretch out your hand and I'll pull you in. You can bear it. You've got toughness in you, Betsy! Now swim! Swim to me! Live!"

After hearing her friend's words, Betsy caught her second wind. She kept pushing until she was within reach of Redflower. Redflower shouted, "Give me your hand!" As the two hands locked together, Betsy felt relief. She was safe, and she had given it all she had. With the aid of Redflower, she made it.

Betsy fell at the feet of Redflower, exhausted. As she tried to gather herself, Redflower said, "Maybe next time you won't run your mouth off to me. Boast all you want to others! Lie and brag to them, but not to me!"

"Yes, Redflower," was all that Betsy could muster.

Redflower, seeing her friend had learned her lesson, said, "We will speak of it no more. Let us go and dry off. Are you hungry Betsy?"

"Yes, I am. I like to eat. I'm always hungry," Betsy said with fresh energy.

Redflower then put her arms around Betsy and hugged her.

Some days later, the medicine man who kicked Redflower out of the tribe, was collecting plants and herbs. Redflower spotted him. She warned, "Stay here Betsy. I have a debt to pay to La Koonish the medicine man. This doesn't concern you."

But Betsy wanted to help protect her. She protested, "I want to help you Redflower. I want to be by your side. If you leave, then I leave. If you fight, then I fight. If you eat, then I eat. If you sleep, then I sleep. My life is with you always."

Hearing how Betsy felt about her, Redflower was moved to tears.

Redflower said, "Then let us settle the score together. First, we must put on our war paint. Betsy, paint me first, then I'll paint you." Redflower taught Betsy how to put on traditional war paint. There were three stripes on Redflower's face and two stripes on Betsy's face- fewer stripes for Betsy, because she was the youngest. As the two females stalked their prey, La Koonish did not yet realize it.

Redflower laid out her plan to Betsy, "Hide behind this rock, and I will lay low behind the bushes. When he comes near us we will spring up and surprise him. I promise you, Betsy, that this day he will not escape us. I will make him pay for what he did to me."

La Koonish declared Redflower was a living curse upon the tribe. He beat her and vowed to wipe out her entire family. La Koonish had Redflower's father stoned to death for bringing Redflower into the world. Redflower's mother was sentenced to be buried in the ground with only her head sticking out. La Koonish then put honey all over her head, so that the ants could eat her alive. La Koonish killed every member of Redflower's family. But he wanted to keep Redflower alive so she could suffer for the rest of her life. He wanted her to feel the hurt and remember his hatred toward Redflower and all of her blood relatives.

Hearing this story, Betsy felt sad for Redflower. Betsy had felt a similar pain because she, too, lost her grandfather and all her friends to the masked men. Betsy felt that she and Redflower had a lot in common. Redflower was her family now. Betsy was so glad that Redflower came into her life. Without Redflower, Betsy would never have survived.

Feeling Redflower's pain and anguish, Betsy said, "I am so very, very sorry Redflower. I can feel your pain. Let us make him pay."

Soon, the two girls were ready to attack. With the anger and anguish boiling, La Koonish felt the girls' presence. His heart told him to run.

"Oh no, you don't!" said Redflower. "You wiped out my entire family."

Fear came to La Koonish's face, and he tried to lie to save himself, "I don't know you. I am a good man. Please let me go. I am a good man. I will do you no harm."

"Shut up!" Redflower protested. "How dare you lie to me. You're not a good man. You're a wicked man who must pay with your life today. My little brother, you threw off a cliff. My father, you stoned. And my poor little mother, you buried in the ground and let the ants eat her. Run, La Koonish." She let him have a head start because she didn't want him to die easily. "Run, you coward! Try to save yourself. Your sorry life isn't worth anything!"

The family killer tried to escape. He ran and he ran. But the two young females were right behind him. The more he ran, the more the girls laughed. Redflower shouted, "Are you tired? I hope so, La Koonish. Does it hurt? How are your lungs? Can you breathe? How are your legs? Do they hurt?"

As Redflower and Betsy moved closer, La Koonish knew he didn't have much time left. He stopped, got on his knees, and pleaded for his life.

"Don't beg, you coward!" Redflower shouted. With one strong kick, he fell to the ground. She told Betsy it was done. "Now I'm satisfied. I'm not a wicked person, but there was justice today."

La Koonish glared at her in excruciating pain.

Redflower said, "You made me feel the greatest pain of all. You took away my family and my love.

My heart is broken. Before you draw your last breath confess!"

"I'm suffering!" shouted La Koonish. "I…am… suffering."

Redflower shouted, "Does it hurt?"

"Yes…it does." La Koonish whimpered.

"Keep on suffering," said Redflower. Blood was running from La Koonish's mouth.

Betsy didn't like the sight of blood. She said, "Redflower, let us go from this place. Your people might be looking for him, and we can't fight them all. Not the whole tribe. If they catch up with us, they will have our head on a spear."

Redflower heard those words and knew Betsy was right, but before leaving, Redflower took one look back at the man who had caused her so much pain. She could finally let go.

The two warriors headed home. Redflower felt justice was served. She could live knowing that her family was avenged. On this day, she fought for the honor of her family. La Koonish would never kill any-one else again. As the two got home near the water, they could not put what they were feeling into words. There was silence for the whole day.

Eventually, the heavy emotions subsided. Redflower and Betsy started to talk about life again. As the two lay on their backs and looked at the stars above, Redflower thought aloud, "Things are chang-ing in my land. It will never be the same. The old ways of the West are dying out. Soon my people will have to make changes in their lives, too, because this country has foreigners coming in. Tell me about your people, Betsy. Why were they slaves in my land? You say your people are from Africa. Why were they brought over here?"

Betsy thought for a moment. After a while, she said, "Well, I will tell you, Redflower. People who wanted to make a profit needed cheap labor. If you can make slaves out of people, you get free labor. My people were brought over to your land to work for the slave owners, the Europeans. I hated the Europeans for this. However, some of my people were sold to Europeans by other members of my own people. This made me realize that there's good and bad in every race. Make no mistake, there are still good Europeans that hated slavery. I've come to realize that. This is life."

Redflower wondered how people could be so evil. She said, "So that's how the blacks were brought here. To work for labor as slaves. To make a profit for the slave owners…your people were taken against their will too?"

Betsy nodded yes.

"This is not right," Redflower said. "But your people are free now, free from the evil Europeans."

Betsy looked at Redflower with a frown. "Free?" Betsy said with confusion. "What freedom? My people went out West to get a fresh start. Look what happened to my grandfather and the rest of my people. The cowardly men that wore masks massacred all of them. Despite that, I still want you to understand not all Europeans were like the masked men. Back in the fields, abolitionists would come to help us. They hated slavery and the mistreatment of blacks. So, Redflower, always have an open mind. There's good and bad everywhere. Look what La Koonish did to your family. He is of your people. Now let us speak of this no more. It pains me to know that life can be so cruel. The suffering of your people and mine make me sick."

The two girls were appreciative to have their lives but cried themselves to sleep thinking about the pain they had experienced.

The next day, Redflower and Betsy were walking to hunt when they heard the cry of a woman's voice. "Help, somebody!" the woman called out.

"Shut up!" said a man's voice. "Or I'll make you shut up!" The voice sounded familiar to Betsy.

Redflower and Betsy crawled on the ground to remain unnoticed. Getting a better view, Betsy and Redflower noticed the woman's husband was tied to a wagon wheel. A woman holding a small baby was trapped between two rocks. A humongous man with a vicious dog was holding the woman against her will.

As the large man looked at the woman with desire, he said, "First I'm going to do what I want to you, and I'll make your husband watch. Then I will chop him up nice and slow and make YOU watch."

"You're evil!" said the woman.

With a loud laugh, the large man said, "You're right. I am."

All of a sudden, the vicious dog smelled something - the two girls hiding on the ground. As the large man looked around to see why the dog was barking, Betsy recognized him as one of the men who wore a mask, one of the men that killed her grandfather! She would never forget his disgusting laugh. Curiosity turned to rage for Betsy.

The dog started to bark louder at the two brave females, but the sound of the dog did not frighten them. The large man said, "Do you smell something boy? Get it! Bring it to me." The dog obeyed his master, running to investigate what he smelled.

As the dog approached the two girls, he snarled like a vicious animal. But as he got closer, the dog fell completely silent. Out of the blue, the dog whirled through the air like a stone skipped across the water. The poor creature's neck was broken by Redflower.

The odds were now in the girl's favor. Fearfully, the man called out, "I am armed. You better come out or I'll do something bad to the woman and the baby!"

Her husband, still tied to the wagon wheel, said, "Let me go you coward!"

The large man slapped the woman's helpless husband in the face and told him to shut up. "You're the next one to be done away with," the large man threatened. The beast of a man walked toward what was hiding near the bushes on the ground. He cocked his gun. Come out! I said come out!"

"Come and get us," said Redflower.

Upon hearing the sound of a female voice, the large man grew confident. He said, "Woman, you're in big trouble. If you give up now, I will finish you so quickly that you won't suffer long. You killed my dog. So now you're going to pay."

Redflower looked at Betsy and whispered very softly, "Spread out, and we will attack him before he knows what hit him."

The man said, "You won't come out, so I'm coming in with no mercy!"

Before the rotten, useless large husk of a person could act, Redflower and Betsy came out of nowhere to meet the enemy with fire in their eyes.

The large man finally saw the two girls. They moved like warriors. A look of shock came upon his face. The man was no match for them. One went at his legs, and the other went at his chest. The man was felled and dropped to the ground. Redflower looked at the large man, cowering on the ground. "Does it hurt?" She shouted. He was too injured to speak.

Redflower then looked at the woman with the baby and her husband before turning to leave. Redflower said, "Free your husband."

The woman replied, "I am forever grateful that you saved me and my husband. Please don't go. Who are you and your little friend?"

"I am Redflower, and her name is Betsy," Redflower quickly answered. "But we must leave. And so should you. This is a bad place. This is enemy country. Many bad men come through here looking for people traveling alone."

"But will you go with us?" The woman said.

"No," answered Redflower." We must go our own way."

The woman, still shaken up, said, "How do we go West?"

Redflower instructed, "See the sunset?"

"Yes," said the woman.

"Follow the sunset, and it will guide you West."

The husband and the woman could not thank the girls enough for saving them. Redflower then realized what Betsy meant when she said that there's good in all kinds of people no matter what they look like.

"If we ever meet again, you are most welcome in our house," said the man and the woman.

Redflower said, "We probably will never meet again, but I will say this. You should turn his bad man over to the authorities. But first, tie him up. If he was dead, we would leave him for the vultures and the dogs, for he does not deserve a burial."

Betsy then said, "Even the buzzards might get sick from eating this nasty person. His carcass does not even have enough worth for a dog to consume."

Redflower laughed and said, "Let us go from this place."

They both wished the man and woman safe travels and a good life. Redflower and Betsy could not stand by and watch a person be tortured. Just standing by reminded them too much of their own families.

As Redflower and Betsy left the territory, they came upon swampland. All of a sudden, they heard the moaning of a dog. It was Scarface. Scarface was in trouble and was stuck in quicksand. Redflower said,

"Well, well, well, what do we have here? Somebody's in trouble."

But Betsy said, "I know you're angry at Scarface, but I think he's learned his lesson. Let's pull him out of the quicksand. Maybe someday he'll be our ally."

"I don't trust him," said Redflower.

"But we have to give him a chance," said Betsy.

Redflower stepped away while Betsy took the initiative to get a rope and pull Scarface out of the quicksand. Once Scarface was freed, he shook himself off of the quicksand mud, briefly looked at the two girls, kept his distance, and then just took off. Betsy felt like Scarface had an expression of gratitude. This time he did not bother to attack them.

"Well, you certainly took a chance," said Redflower.

Betsy said, "Well, sometimes you have to take chances in life to do the right thing. Enough about Scarface. It's time to go and see other parts of the land. It's a beautiful day to go hunting. Can I lead this time?"

"Yeah, I want some fish," said Redflower. "How about you, Betsy?"

"Yes, I want some fish too. I must say I'm quite hungry. Until our next adventure, we'll go fishing and just relax. And I'll bet I can catch more than you! Let us go!"

About the Author

Jonathan Beard is a guy from Michigan who always enjoyed writing stories.